The Yearbook & The Impala

Something In The Water — Books One and Two

Lorri Ryan Oliver

Tribury Media LLC
Middlebury, Connecticut

Published by Tribury Media LLC, Middlebury, Connecticut
This is a work of fiction. Names, characters, places and incidents are products of the author's imagination or are used fictitiously.

This is a work of original fiction. The author used standard digital tools, including AI, for research, continuity, story development, and editing.

Lorri Ryan Oliver is a pen name.

ISBN: 979-8-9953431-3-4
First Edition, 2026
Also available as an ebook wherever ebooks are sold.
This story begins here.

Read slowly. Step over nothing.

The Bottle

He called on a Wednesday.

I was in the office at Amorous, which is the restaurant I own in Thornbury, Connecticut, doing the thing I do on Wednesday afternoons when the restaurant is closed and the building is mine - sitting at my desk with a glass of water and a spreadsheet, pretending that running a business is the same as understanding one. The phone rang with a Stamford area code, which I almost didn't answer because Stamford area codes usually mean someone is trying to sell me a new credit card processor.

"Is this Lorri Oliver?"

"It is."

"This is going to sound strange."

It did sound strange. A man's voice - pleasant, a little nervous, the kind of nervous that comes from rehearsing a phone call in your car before making it. He told me his name and said he'd graduated from Wright Tech in 1981. Electrical shop. He said he'd found me on Classmates.com, where I'd posted a profile six months earlier for no particular reason except that I was sixty years old and had started doing things for no particular reason.

I'd written that I was in food trades at Wright Tech but didn't graduate. That I was a recent widow. That if you searched hard enough, you'd find a magazine article about a restaurant in Thornbury. I'd thought it was a message in a bottle. Apparently someone found the bottle.

He'd found the article. He'd found the restaurant. He'd done more internet detective work than I'd expected from a man who spent three years learning to wire junction boxes. And now he was on the phone asking if he could stop by sometime.

"Come Friday," I said. "Nine-thirty. Things calm down around here by then."

I hung up and sat with my hand on the phone for a moment, the way you do when you've just agreed to something and you're not sure what it is yet.

I should tell you what I knew about this man, because it wasn't much. We'd been at Wright Tech at the same time - 1979 to 1981. He was in electrical, I was in food trades. Different shops, different worlds. We shared a cafeteria and whatever common spaces existed between the smell of solder and the smell of onions. I remembered sitting in his car once with other kids, radio on, the kind of aimless afternoon that felt like freedom when you were seventeen. I wouldn't have called us friends. I wouldn't have called us anything. We were classmates who occupied the same three years and then went in different directions - he toward graduation and I toward something else entirely, which is a story I don't tell at dinner parties.

That was forty-three years ago. I'd built an entire life since then - married Colin, raised two daughters, worked thirty-three years at the Restaurant Buyers Association selling kitchen equipment to every chef in Fairfield and Litchfield County, buried Colin, sold the house, bought a building, and opened a restaurant. Forty-three years of becoming a person he'd never met, and now he wanted to come see the person I'd become on a Friday night in November.

I said yes because I was curious. I want to be clear about that. Not lonely, not desperate, not scanning the horizon for male companionship. Curious. A man from 1981 had gone looking for me, and I wanted to know what he expected to find.

* * *

Friday came the way November Fridays do in Connecticut - early dark, the smell of cold air, the promise of weather. By nine o'clock the last diners were settling their checks and Richard was starting his closing routine. Richard Wilkins is my partner at Amorous, a former colleague from my years at the Association. He runs the front of house when I'm not there and supports the kitchen when I am, and on most nights he does both of these things while somehow also knowing exactly when to disappear.

Martin had already cleaned his station and gone home. Martin Hale is my chef - a man who has cooked in Connecticut kitchens for thirty years and has never once needed you to know his name. He leaves when the kitchen closes and he arrives when it opens and the hours between are his own business.

Ginny was behind the bar, polishing a glass. Ginny Rettig is my bartender. She sees everything, says almost nothing, and what she says tends to arrive with the quiet finality of a door closing. She'd been with me since the opening and had developed an almost supernatural ability to read my mood from the way I adjusted the lighting.

"You changed the sconces twice," she said without looking up.

"I'm adjusting the room."

"You adjusted it an hour ago."

I had. The restaurant was empty now except for the three of us, and I'd been fiddling with the dimmers since eight-thirty, trying to find the right balance between "intimate" and "I can still read a yearbook." The pink-tinted sconces along the walls gave everything a warm glow that made the wood look older and the people look younger, which was the point of them. The four industrial pendants over the bar cast focused pools of light on the dark wood surface, leaving the back-bar in amber shadow. The tin ceiling above caught the light and held it.

I'd dressed carefully, which I told myself was professional. The restaurant owner greeting a guest. A fitted white blouse - not the satin one I save for occasions I haven't invented yet, but a good cotton broadcloth with darts that acknowledged I had a figure worth acknowledging. A charcoal skirt that fell past my knees. Low heels, not the four-inch platforms that lived in the back of my closet waiting for a reason. My hair was down, reddish-brown, curling past my shoulders. I'd put on lipstick. I'd taken it off. I'd put it on again.

Ginny noticed this too, because Ginny noticed everything.

"He's a classmate," I said. "From Wright Tech. Forty-three years ago."

"Okay."

"He found me on Classmates.com."

"Okay."

"He's bringing his yearbook."

Ginny set the glass down on the bar. The sound was very precise. "His yearbook."

"His 1981 yearbook. He wants to show me his class photos."

Ginny picked up another glass. "A man in his sixties is driving to Thornbury on a snowy Friday night to show you his high school yearbook."

"It's not snowing yet."

"It will be."

Nine-Thirty

She was right. It started around nine-fifteen - fat, slow flakes that drifted past the windows and caught the light from the parking lot. By nine-thirty, Route 6 had a thin white coat and the world outside looked like a photograph someone had softened on purpose.

He arrived at nine-thirty exactly. I heard the door - the outer door to the vestibule, then the inner glass door - and then he was standing at the host stand, shaking snow off a black wool car coat, and I was walking toward him.

He was carrying a yearbook. Burgundy cover. 1981. He held it against his chest the way you hold something you've brought a long distance and don't want to damage.

I looked at him and did the math that everyone does when they see someone they knew at seventeen and haven't seen since. The hair was different - shorter, lighter, gray at the temples. The face had settled into itself, the way men's faces do, losing the softness of youth and gaining something that reads as either authority or fatigue depending on the lighting. Blue eyes. Clean-shaven. A few wrinkles, the kind that come from laughing or squinting or both. Dark wool pants, a pin-striped shirt under a V-neck sweater, black loafers. He looked like a man who had spent time in front of a mirror before driving here, which is the same thing I had done, which meant we were both pretending this was casual and neither of us believed it.

"Lorri," he said.

"Hi," I said. The word came out softer than I intended.

We stood there for a moment, doing the recalibration. He was taller than I remembered - or I'd forgotten. He smelled like cold air and something woodsy, a cologne that was present without announcing itself. I extended my hand and he took it, and the handshake lasted a beat longer than handshakes usually do.

"You look exactly the same," he said, which was not true but was the right thing to say.

"You look like you survived," I said, which made him laugh, which was what I wanted.

I showed him to the corner booth - the red leather one, the one I'd had installed because I wanted at least one piece of furniture in this restaurant that looked like it had a story. He slid in across from me and set the yearbook on the table between us. Burgundy cover. Gold lettering. Wright Technical School, 1981.

"You brought it," I said.

"I told you I would."

"I know. I just didn't think you'd actually -" I stopped. "Never mind. I'm glad you did."

Ginny materialized with two glasses of water and a look that communicated everything. She took our order - Kahlua on the rocks for both of us, which seemed right for a November night - and disappeared.

He opened the yearbook.

* * *

We spent an hour with that yearbook. He turned pages and pointed to faces and told me who they were - the ones he'd stayed in touch with, the ones he'd lost track of, the ones who'd become legends in the way that people from your hometown become legends when you're far enough away to mythologize them. I knew some of the faces. Most I didn't.

He found his own picture. Shop photo - the electrical class standing in two rows, sixteen young men in work shirts squinting into a flash. He was in the back row. Thin, dark-haired, the particular serious expression that seventeen-year-old boys adopt when they want to look older than they are.

"That's you," I said.

"That was me," he said. "Forty-three years and about thirty pounds ago."

"You look like you're trying to be serious."

"I was always trying to be serious. It never took."

He found the food trades section. My class. I was in the front row, second from the left, in a white chef's coat that was slightly too big for me because I'd borrowed it from a girl who was slightly larger. My hair was longer then - down to the middle of my back, which I'd forgotten. I was smiling the way you smile when someone tells you to smile.

His finger went to the caption first, not to the picture. He found the names along the bottom, second from left, and stopped there.

"Lorri Ryan," he said.

Then he looked up at me. Not at the photograph. At me.

His finger stayed where it was.

After a moment it moved, slowly, up to the girl in the front row.

"There you are."

I looked at the girl in the photograph. I'd been seventeen. I'd been a string bean in a borrowed coat, and in eight months I'd leave this school and not go back and spend the next forty-three years becoming someone else entirely. The girl in the photograph didn't know any of that yet.

"I look young," I said.

"You were young."

"We were both young." I looked at him. "Strange, isn't it? That we were in the same building for three years and now we're sitting here."

"I thought about you," he said. "More than you probably knew."

I looked at him steadily. "Why didn't you say anything?"

He considered this. "Seventeen," he said finally. "I didn't know how."

The Kahlua arrived. Ginny set the glasses down without a word and went back to the bar. The restaurant was quiet - just us and the low music and the snow moving past the windows.

The jingle of harness bells cut through the muffled quiet of the snowfall. We both looked up as a horse-drawn sleigh glided past the window on Main Street, the horse's breath visible in the cold.

"Only in Thornbury," I said.

He laughed. "That's not a thing that happens in regular towns?"

"Not anymore. Thornbury keeps the Mayberry alive."

We kept turning pages. He found the football team. He'd played - offensive line, which explained something about the shoulders. He found the drama club, which he hadn't joined but which contained three girls he'd been secretly in love with. He found the shop awards page, where his name appeared under Electrical Excellence, which made me laugh.

"Electrical Excellence," I said. "Very distinguished."

"I could wire your entire restaurant right now," he said. "If you needed it."

"I'll keep that in mind."

We were leaning in over the yearbook by then, our heads close together over the pages, and I was aware of the proximity in the way you become aware of proximity when it's been a while since you've been close to someone. He smelled good. His arm was warm against mine on the table. He turned a page and his hand brushed mine and neither of us moved away.

He kissed me. I didn't see it coming - or I did, and I'd decided not to interfere. He leaned in and kissed me once, very briefly, the way you test whether something is allowed. Then he pulled back and looked at me.

I looked back at him.

"Okay," I said.

* * *

I kissed him. This time it was me. I leaned in and found his mouth and kissed him with intention, and he responded, and we stayed there for a while - long enough that the yearbook became irrelevant, long enough that my hand found his chest and his hand found my shoulder and then my back, and the space between us dissolved into warmth and pressure and the taste of Kahlua and something underneath that was just him.

When we came up for air, the yearbook was still open to the football team.

"We should keep looking at this," I said.

"We should," he said, not moving his hand from my back.

We did. We turned pages and kissed between pages and turned more pages and kissed between those. His hand stayed on my back, then moved to my waist, then back to my shoulder. My hand rested on his thigh, then on the yearbook, then on his arm. We migrated around each other the way you do when you're not following a plan - just finding where your hand wants to be next.

He pointed to a picture of the cafeteria. "That's where I used to sit."

"I sat by the windows."

"I know. I remember."

"You remember where I sat in the cafeteria forty-three years ago?"

"You were hard to miss, Lorri."

I laughed. "I was a string bean."

"You were memorable."

I kissed him for that, and this time his hand found my waist and stayed there, and I felt the warmth of his palm through the fabric of my blouse, and something inside me shifted - not dramatically, not with fireworks, but the way a season shifts, so gradually you don't notice until suddenly the light is different and you can't remember when it changed.

We spent an hour and a half in that booth. I know because I looked at the clock when we sat down and I looked at it when we stood up and the math said ninety minutes but the experience said something else - something shorter and longer at the same time, the way time works when you're not monitoring it.

We kissed. We talked. We turned pages. We kissed more. His hand rested on my chest at one point - not my breast, my chest. Above everything, on my sternum, over my heartbeat. The placement was either instinct or accident and it doesn't matter which. What matters is that he touched the person, not the body. I felt his palm register my heartbeat and I felt my heartbeat register his palm and I thought: oh. That's what that is.

His hands were gentle. Tentative. The hands of a man who wasn't sure how much he was allowed and wasn't going to push past whatever line existed. I didn't define the line because I didn't know where it was. I was discovering it in real time, the way you discover the edge of a pool in the dark - by feel, by temperature change, by the sudden awareness that you've gone further than you expected and the water is warm.

We talked the entire time. That's what I want you to understand. This wasn't silence and groping. This was two people who'd shared three years of cafeteria banter and then lost each other for forty-three years trying to fill in the gap while also discovering that their bodies still worked and that the combination of memory and touch and Kahlua and snow falling past the window was doing something to both of us that neither of us had planned.

He told me about his kids. I told him about mine. He told me about his work - electrical contracting, his own business, commercial jobs mostly. I told him about the years at the Association, about learning restaurants from the supply side, about the day I decided to stop selling kitchens and start running one. He listened the way men listen when they're actually listening, which is rarer than it should be.

Between the talking, we kissed. Between the kissing, his hands found me - my back, my waist, my shoulder, my hair. And I found him - his chest, his arm, the side of his face. Nothing urgent. Nothing frantic. Just the slow accumulation of touch between two people who had forty-three years of not-touching to account for.

At some point I became aware that Ginny had turned off the bar lights. The restaurant was dark except for the booth candle and the sconces I'd dimmed to their lowest setting. She'd left without saying goodnight, which was the most Ginny thing she could have done - she'd read the room, decided the room didn't need a bartender anymore, and disappeared. I'd find out later she'd locked the front door on her way out and left the key on the bar.

It was almost eleven when we stood up. The yearbook went with us. He carried it the same way he'd carried it in - against his chest, protective, precious. I walked him to the vestibule, where his black wool coat and totes hung on the hooks.

The coat room was small - four feet by six, barely enough for two people standing. He put on his coat and I watched him do it, and then he turned to me in that small space and we kissed one more time. A goodbye kiss. Then another goodbye kiss. Then a third that lasted longer than the first two combined, standing up, coats in the way, his hands on my waist, my hands on his lapels, the yearbook pressed between us because he was still holding it and neither of us was willing to put it down.

It was almost innocent. Almost exactly like saying goodnight on a porch after a date when you were seventeen and your parents were waiting inside and you had to go but you kept not going because the kissing was good and the night was cold and going inside meant it was over.

He left. I watched him walk to his car through the snow, which had accumulated enough to leave footprints. He drove away and his taillights disappeared down Route 6 and I stood in the vestibule for a moment, alone, in a restaurant I'd built from a dream I'd carried for thirty years, and I thought about what had just happened.

I didn't think about whether we'd see each other again. He had a family. He lived nearby. This was probably a one-time thing, and we both knew it without saying it, the way adults know things.

I thought instead about how it felt. The kiss at the host stand. The hand on my chest. The yearbook open between us. The snow. The Kahlua. The way ninety minutes can contain an entire adolescence you never had, returned to you at sixty in a booth you didn't know was built for this.

More

I locked up. I drove home to Middlebury in the snow. I went to bed.

I woke up the next morning and I did not regret a single moment.

That's not nothing, at sixty. Waking up after an unplanned evening with a man you barely knew and feeling not shame, not confusion, not the anxious inventory of what did I do and what does it mean. Just warmth. Just the memory of his hand on my chest and my heartbeat underneath it. Just the thought, quiet and clear as the morning light on the snow outside my window:

More.

Not more of him, specifically. More of this. More of being alive in my body. More of discovering that the woman I'd become had not, in fact, stopped wanting to be touched. More of sitting in a booth with the lights low and the snow falling and a man's hands remembering what hands are for.

I didn't know yet what I would build from that feeling. I didn't know about the booth, about the lighting, about the system that would come later - the careful orchestration, the architecture of encounter and reveal. I didn't know that Ginny would become my accomplice, or that the coat room would become a recurring character, or that I would learn to dress for these evenings the way a chef plates a meal - with intention, with craft, with the understanding that presentation is half the gift.

All of that came later.

That morning, all I knew was that something had woken up. Something I'd put to sleep when I married Colin and raised my daughters and worked my thirty-three years and lived my dutiful life in the house in Redding. Something dormant. Something patient. Something that had waited, quietly, for a man with a yearbook and a snowy Friday night and the simple, ridiculous courage to kiss a woman he barely knew because he'd driven forty miles to show her his football pictures and he couldn't think of another way to say what he meant.

I made coffee. I stood at the kitchen window. The snow from last night was perfect and untouched on the lawn.

More, I thought.

And I smiled.

Threekisses

The coffee was ready before I was.

I'd set the timer the night before — a habit from thirty-three years of early mornings and association meetings and the kind of life that requires you to be somewhere before you're fully awake. The pot had done its job and was waiting for me on the counter, patient, unremarkable, entirely unaware that the woman reaching for it was not the same woman who'd programmed it fourteen hours earlier.

I poured a cup. I stood at the kitchen window.

The snow from last night was perfect and untouched on the lawn. Not the thin, apologetic snow of early November — real snow, the kind that commits. The birdbath had a white hat. The fence posts each wore their own. The lawn looked like a sentence before anyone has written on it.

I thought about his coat.

Black wool, good quality, the kind of coat a man buys when he's done with cheap coats. It had been hanging on the hook in my vestibule for ninety minutes while we sat in the booth and turned pages, and when he put it on at the end it still had the cold in it — the November cold he'd walked in with — and I'd felt it when his hands found my waist and pulled me in for the second goodbye kiss, the wool against my arms, cold on the outside and warm where he was.

Three kisses.

The first one was a question. The second one was an answer. The third one was the one neither of us had planned, the one that started as a goodbye and became something else — longer, slower, his hands on my waist, my hands on his lapels, the yearbook pressed between us because he was still holding it and I wasn't going to be the one to suggest he put it down.

I sipped my coffee. Outside, nothing moved. The snow held everything still.

Here is what I understood that morning that I hadn't understood the night before:

I had built the booth without knowing what I was building.

I thought I was building a restaurant. I thought the corner booth with the red leather and the slatted screen and the plant that blocked the sightline — I thought that was atmosphere. Interior design. The kind of detail that made food writers use words like *intimate* and *considered*. I had not understood, until a man with a 1981 yearbook sat across from me in that booth and put his hand on my blouse, just below my collar, that I had been building something else entirely.

A permission space. A room inside a room.

I'd dimmed the lights to read a yearbook. The lights had other ideas.

Not the moral accounting. I was done with that before I went to sleep. The other kind — the inventory of sensation, the cataloguing of what had actually happened in that booth, what it had meant, what it was for.

His hand, just below the collar, just above everything else. The placement so specific and so right that I'd thought, in the moment: *oh. He knows something.*

Maybe he didn't. Maybe it was instinct, or accident, or the geometry of two people discovering how to sit close after forty-three years of not sitting close at all. It doesn't matter. What matters is that I felt his palm register my heartbeat and I felt my heartbeat register his palm, and for a moment the question of what this was and what it meant and what happened next went entirely quiet.

That's what that is, I had thought.

That's what being touched is, when it's done right.

I stood at the window and did the accounting.

I thought about the yearbook.

Burgundy cover. Gold lettering. He'd carried it against his chest when he arrived, protective, like something fragile. It had sat open between us for ninety minutes and then left with him the same way it came — held carefully, not damaged, returned safely to wherever yearbooks live when they're not doing what that one had just done.

I'd looked at my picture in it. 1981. A girl who didn't graduate, who went somewhere else entirely, who couldn't have told you at seventeen that forty-three years later she would own a restaurant and stand in its vestibule in low heels with a man's cold coat against her arms and not regret any of it — not the leaving, not the years, not the standing there.

Not a single moment.

More, I thought.

Not more of him. More of this. More of the booth and the candle and the third goodbye kiss and the cold coat and the snow and the standing at the window the next morning knowing I had built something I hadn't known I was building.

More of being wanted. More of deciding what I wanted back.

I finished the coffee. I put the mug in the sink. I stood at the window one more moment, looking at the snow, at the fence posts in their white caps, at the lawn like a sentence before anyone has written on it.

Then I went to get dressed.

I had things to build.

The Impala

Something In The Water — Book Two

The Car Show

The car show flyer was taped to the community board at LaBonne's, between a notice about a lost tortoiseshell cat and an advertisement for a piano teacher in Woodbury. I'd been buying cheese and had no particular plans for the following Sunday, which is the only condition under which a woman my age stops at a community board. I stood there with my wheels of Manchego and read the flyer twice.

Woodbury Lions Club Car Show. Hollow Park. Over 400 vehicles. Beer garden.

I called Gia from the parking lot.

* * *

Gia Cummings and I go back far enough that I don't remember meeting her. She was simply there — in Glenbrook, in the way that certain people are fixtures of your childhood before you're old enough to choose your own fixtures. We grew up a few streets apart, fell in and out of touch the way people do across forty years of marriages and moves and lives that don't leave room for maintenance, and then discovered approximately two years ago that we'd both ended up in the same corner of Connecticut without consulting each other about it.

This is the kind of coincidence that stops feeling like coincidence after a while.

Gia is the friend you call when you want to go somewhere and not think too hard about why. She doesn't require agendas. She requires a nice day and the possibility of something happening, which is a different thing entirely, and she brings red nails and a tight top to every occasion regardless of the occasion. She said yes to the car show before I finished the sentence.

We went in sweatshirts and jeans. Hers was fitted. Mine was not. It was a Sunday in October, cool and brilliant, the kind of Connecticut autumn day that makes you understand why people write poems about Connecticut autumns, and we drove to Hollow Park with the windows cracked and the heat on and talked about nothing in particular, which is its own kind of luxury.

* * *

Hollow Park on car show Sunday is a different geography than Hollow Park on any other day. Four hundred vehicles arranged across the grass in long gleaming rows, chrome catching the October light, paint jobs in colors that don't exist on anything built after 1975. The smell of exhaust and funnel cake and something from the beer garden that might have been Reverie Brewing. A DJ somewhere playing Yacht Rock — Christopher Cross, if I'm remembering correctly, which I probably am because "Sailing" is not a song that leaves your memory easily once it arrives.

We paid our ten dollars at the gate and walked in and became part of it.

Gia was immediately at home. She is always immediately at home. Within four minutes she had a beer from the garden tent and was talking to a man in a Woodbury Lions Club vest about the Puerto Rican food truck, and I had lost her completely, which was fine because losing Gia at a car show is like losing a golden retriever at a dog park. She's happy, she's social, she'll find you when she's ready.

I walked the rows. This is what you do at a car show — you walk slowly and read the signs and look at the cars and remember things. Each vehicle has a placard identifying the make, model, year, and owner. The older the car, the more it functions as a kind of time travel, the steel and glass and chrome holding the shape of some specific year when someone decided this was what the world should look like.

I found myself lingering at the older ones. A 1957 Bel Air the color of a swimming pool. A 1969 Mustang that had been restored to within an inch of its original life. A 1972 Chevelle that smelled, improbably, of someone's father.

And then, at the end of a row near the far edge of the park, a 1960 Chevrolet Impala convertible. Fire engine red. White convertible top, folded back on a day that deserved it. Red leather interior, the stitching lying with the precise tension of something that had been done by someone who understood the work. The chrome gleamed with the particular intensity of something that has been cared for meticulously by someone who understands that caring for things is not the same as being precious about them.

I read the sign.

1960 Chevrolet Impala. Owner: Wayne Xavier. Acquired: 1980.

I read it twice. Then I looked up.

He was standing fifteen feet away, talking to another man about something under a nearby hood. Dark hair, salt-and-pepper, the natural curl of it. Weathered face. Clean-shaven. A flannel shirt and jeans and work boots, the outfit of a man who dresses for the day he's actually having. He hadn't noticed me yet.

Wayne Xavier. Wright Tech, 1979 to 1981. Auto shop. I was food trades. Different shops, different worlds — we shared a cafeteria and whatever common spaces existed between the smell of motor oil and the smell of onions. I'd been one of the onion half.

He'd taken me to the Norwalk Drive-In once, in the summer of 1980. A group of us, though I recalled it narrowing to just the two of us at some point in the evening. We'd kissed a little. Touched a little. Nothing came of it — that was a summer of other complications, and a boy at a drive-in was sweet but not what I was managing.

Forty-three years. I stood next to his Impala and did the math and felt it land.

He turned from the conversation and saw me. The recognition arrived in stages — the slight narrowing of his eyes, the tilt of the head, the moment the filing system produces the right folder. Then his face opened into a smile.

"Lorri."

"Wayne Xavier," I said. "That the same car?"

He looked at the Impala the way people look at things they've spent years with — not admiringly, exactly, but with a private acknowledgment. "Since 1980. Bought it junior year, used. Kept it ever since."

I looked at the red leather seats, the stitching, the way the material lay with the precise tension of someone who understood its properties. "You did the interior yourself."

"How'd you know?"

"Because it looks like someone who knew what they were doing did it."

He seemed pleased by this in a way that wasn't performance. "Upholstery. That's my trade."

"I know. I remember."

He looked at me for a moment. "You look exactly like yourself."

"That's either a compliment or a neutral observation," I said.

"Compliment," he said, without hesitation.

* * *

Gia found us twenty minutes later, which is Gia's version of giving someone space. She arrived with two more beers and a paper basket of something from the food truck and assessed the situation in approximately one second, which is how long it takes Gia to assess any situation involving a man and a woman standing close together next to a beautiful car.

"Gia Cummings," I said. "Wayne Xavier. We went to Wright Tech together."

"All three of us?" Gia said.

"Wayne and I. You went to Stamford High."

"I went to Stamford High and I turned out fine," Gia said, and handed Wayne a beer with the ease of someone who has never in her life handed a stranger a beer and had it feel strange.

We found a picnic table near the beer garden. The DJ had moved on to Hall & Oates, which felt appropriate for three people who had been young in approximately the same era. Gia ate her food and asked Wayne questions with the directness of a woman who considers social niceties an inefficient detour, and he answered them with the ease of a man who is comfortable being asked direct questions.

What did he do. Upholstery — custom, mostly cars, semi-retired. He worked out of Stamford, had for thirty years. Where did he live. Stamford, still. Was that his Impala. It was. Since 1980. Gia put her beer down and looked at him.

"You bought that car in high school," she said.

"Junior year."

"And you still have it."

"Still have it."

Gia looked at the Impala, then back at Wayne, with the expression of someone recalibrating an assessment. "That's either very romantic or very stubborn."

"Little of both," Wayne said.

"He did the interior himself," I said.

Gia nodded at this with the approval of someone who respects people who are good at things. "What does a car like that need, interior-wise?"

And Wayne talked about it — briefly, two sentences, the way he talked about things he knew well. The original seat material. What he'd chosen instead, and why. The particular way the red leather had to be cut to follow the bench seat's curve without puckering at the corners. Then he stopped, because that was enough, and went back to his beer.

"He should have won something today," Gia said to me.

"I don't enter to win," Wayne said.

"Why not?"

He considered this. "I know what it is. I don't need a trophy to tell me."

Gia pointed at him with her beer cup. "That's either very zen or very stubborn."

"Little of both," he said again, and smiled.

The afternoon did what October afternoons do when they're behaving well — it stayed golden and cool and the light moved slowly across the park and there was no particular reason to be anywhere else. We talked about the cars and the town and the peculiar fact of finding people you knew in entirely different contexts of your life suddenly living in your backyard. Wayne had his business in Stamford, had been there thirty years. Gia had landed in Southbury. I was in Middlebury, running a restaurant in Thornbury. Three people from Glenbrook-area Stamford, all of us within range of each other, none of us having planned it.

"Something in the water," Gia said.

"Don't say that in Thornbury," I said.

She grinned. She knew the rumor.

Wayne was watching the two of us with the comfortable attention of a man who enjoys a conversation without needing to own it. He wasn't performing — wasn't leaning forward with deliberate charm or steering topics toward himself or doing any of the things men do when they've decided they'd like to make an impression. He was just there. Present and easy and warm, which turned out to be more effective than any of the alternatives.

At one point I said something about the restaurant — about the particular challenge of building a regular clientele in a town that was small enough to be intimate and large enough to be unpredictable — and he listened the way men listen when they're actually processing and not just waiting for their turn. Then he said: "You retired into one."

"Into one what?"

"Restaurant. Thirty-three years selling kitchens. You retired into a kitchen."

I looked at him. "I suppose I did."

"Makes sense," he said. "You learn everything about something for thirty years, you either walk away from it or you go all the way in."

Gia pointed at him with her beer cup. "He's right."

"He is right," I said.

The trophies were presented at three o'clock. Wayne didn't win anything, which he accepted with the equanimity of a man who didn't enter to win. We walked back to his Impala together while Gia drifted toward the Ben & Jerry's tent with the purposefulness of someone who has identified a priority. Wayne put the top up against the cooling afternoon air and we stood and looked at the car in the lowering October light.

"The drive-in," I said. "Summer of '80."

"I wondered if you remembered."

"Norwalk Drive-In. I don't remember what we saw."

"Neither do I," he said.

We stood there for a moment with that comfortable admission between us — two people who remembered the fact of something without remembering its content, which is its own kind of intimacy.

Then something else surfaced. The way things do when you've been standing next to the right object long enough.

"Dover," I said.

He looked at me. "Dover Drag Strip."

"That summer. All four of us."

"You and Gia," he said. "Me and—" He paused. "I don't remember his name."

"Neither do I," I said.

We looked at the Impala. The same car. The summer of 1980, when we were seventeen and the world was loud and fast and Gia had been everywhere at once and a drag strip in New York was just another Saturday and none of us had been keeping careful records.

"Should we tell her?" he said.

I glanced toward the Ben & Jerry's tent. "She won't remember."

"Probably not," he said, with the equanimity of a man who finds this neither surprising nor troubling. "She had a full schedule."

"She had an extremely full schedule," I said.

He smiled. I smiled. Gia emerged from the tent with a cone and a look of profound satisfaction and rejoined us without any idea that she had just been the subject of a forty-three-year-old footnote.

"What?" she said, reading our faces.

"Nothing," I said.

"You were talking about me."

"We were talking about the car," I said.

She looked at the Impala, then at Wayne, then at me. The assessment took one second, as always. "Sure you were," she said, and licked her cone.

* * *

"You should come to Amorous sometime," I said to Wayne, when Gia had drifted again toward the exit and we had a moment. "Bring the car."

He looked at me. "Is that an invitation?"

"It's an observation that has the structure of an invitation."

He smiled. The smile lines deepened around his eyes. "I'll find it."

"It's not on GPS," I said. "Ask someone who knows."

* * *

Between October and May, the Electrician happened. That's Book One, and if you haven't read it, the short version is this: a man I barely knew drove through the snow with a forty-three-year-old yearbook and kissed me at the host stand and we spent ninety minutes in a booth I didn't know was built for that purpose yet, and I drove home and woke up the next morning thinking *more.*

I spent the winter with that word. Turning it over. Understanding what it meant and what it didn't mean and what I was quietly, without blueprints, beginning to build.

By spring I knew.

* * *

Voices Visit

The man from *Voices* had been to every restaurant in the Quadbury region at least twice, and most of them had the decency to look like restaurants. This one looked like someone's grandmother had opened a supper club in her living room and forgotten to tell the sign maker what it was about.

He checked his phone. Amorous Restaurant, Main Street, Thornbury. The address on the business registry didn't match the address on the building, which was either a clerical error or something he'd need to mention in the write-up. He pushed through the glass door into a small vestibule, stepped through the inner door, and hung his jacket in the coat room — curtain pulled open, brass hooks polished so many times they'd lost their corners. He turned into the dining room.

The lighting hit him first. It was twelve-thirty on a Tuesday afternoon and the room was glowing. Not dim exactly — warm. Pink-warm, like the last ten minutes before sunset if sunset happened indoors and never ended. He could see everything in the room but nothing too clearly, which he suspected was the point. Outside, Main Street was doing its bright October thing. In here, October had been politely asked to wait.

A woman behind a small bar looked up from a glass she was polishing and smiled at him the way a person smiles when they've already decided something about you.

"You must be from *Voices*," she said.

"Is it that obvious?"

"You have your notebook out and you haven't sat down yet." She set the glass and cloth on the bar. "Ginny Rettig."

She took two steps to a door behind the bar, knocked once, and came back to her glass.

He looked around while he waited. Eight tables, maybe ten, each with a small candle. A corner booth behind a slatted screen with a plant that blocked the sightline entirely — you'd have to be sitting in it to know who else was. A back bar lined with vinyl records in cubbies, bottles catching the amber light. A vintage amplifier, its twin VU meters dark at this hour — the needles waiting for a record to drop before they'd swing into their slow blue-green pulse. Pink-tinted sconces along the walls, and above everything, a pressed tin ceiling that caught the light and held it like a secret.

He wrote: *Address discrepancy. Unusual name. Pink lighting at noon.*

Then he wrote: *Plant blocking booth. Why.*

"Romantic restaurants like to offer seclusion," said a voice at his elbow.

He turned. A woman in her early sixties stood beside him, dark reddish hair, a gray vest over a white blouse, coffee cup in one hand. With the other she gestured lightly toward the corner booth behind the plant.

"Lorri Oliver," she said, and put out her hand. "You found us."

"Eventually," he said. "The address on the registry—"

"Doesn't match," she said. "I know. The building faces Main Street. The door is on the side. It's been this way since we opened."

"Does that affect business?"

"People who find it come back." She tilted her head. A smile with layers in it. "People who don't find it weren't the right people anyway."

He wrote that down.

* * *

They sat at the bar. He had his notebook open and she had her coffee, and the questions went the way these things go — menu concept, hours, history, what made Amorous different from the other establishments in the Quadbury region.

"The Quadbury region," she repeated. "That's what we are now?"

"*Voices* covers Woodbury, Southbury, Middlebury, Waterbury—"

"And Thornbury."

"And Thornbury."

"The five boroughs," she said, and smiled.

He asked about the name.

"The building needed one," she said. "The building is on Main Street in Thornbury, Connecticut. It has pink lights and a pressed tin ceiling and a corner booth with a plant in front of it." She set down her coffee cup. "What would you have called it?"

He considered this with more seriousness than he'd expected to. "Fair point," he said.

"The food is very good, though," Ginny offered. "Contemporary American. Seasonal. Lorri trained at Wright Tech and spent thirty years in restaurant assessment."

"Thirty years telling other restaurants what they were doing wrong," Lorri said. "Now I get to do it my way. Or at least do it mine."

He wrote that down. "What would you call the concept? Farm to table? Comfort food?"

Lorri looked at Ginny. Ginny looked at Lorri. Something passed between them that was not on the menu.

"The concept," Lorri said, "is that people should enjoy themselves."

"Most restaurants would say that."

"Most restaurants mean the food."

He wrote that down too, then stared at it. He underlined *mean* and wasn't sure why.

"Can I see the kitchen?"

"Of course." Lorri set down her coffee, stepped off her stool, and crossed to the hallway on the right. She said Richard's name once into it, not loud, and came back to her seat.

A moment later a man came out of the hallway drying his hands on a towel. Tall, silver-haired, the kind of bearing that suggested he'd spent decades making other people comfortable in rooms. He looked like he belonged behind a desk at a firm that didn't need to advertise, except for the apron.

"Richard Wilkins, co-owner," he said. "You want the tour?"

"If you don't mind."

"I never mind." Richard tilted his head back the way he'd come. "This way."

The writer followed him down the hallway, past the bathrooms, into the open kitchen entrance — no door, just the opening, the angle hidden from the dining room behind them.

The kitchen was small, clean, and serious. Good equipment — not showy, but the kind of commercial hardware that someone who'd spent thirty years assessing restaurants would know how to buy right. Everything was where it should be. A cutting board with fresh tarragon. The hood system humming. A gratin already browning in the oven and filling the room with something that made the word *lunch* feel like an understatement.

"This is a real kitchen," the man said, and meant it as a compliment.

"What were you expecting?"

"I don't know. The dining room out there is — " He gestured vaguely.

"The dining room is Lorri's," Richard said. He folded the towel once and hung it on a hook. "The kitchen is mine. The food speaks for itself. Out there, Lorri speaks for everything else."

"What does she say?"

Richard looked at him with the patience of a man who'd been asked this before by people who hadn't earned the answer yet. "Stay for lunch," he said. "You'll hear it."

They came back out the way they'd come. Lorri was leaning in to say something to Ginny that made Ginny's eyes go wide and then narrow and then wide again. Whatever it was, it was over by the time the men reached the bar.

"Everything in order back there?" Lorri asked.

"Spotless," the man said. "You'd pass any inspection."

"We do pass every inspection." She tilted her head. The smile came back, the one with the layers. "Was that what you were inspecting?"

"I'm just writing the profile."

"Of course you are." She touched his arm for exactly one second — a hostess touch, nothing more, though it somehow conveyed that she knew the difference between a hostess touch and the other kind, and that the difference was smaller than most people thought. "Stay. Eat. The gratin is almost ready and it's worth the wait."

The chicken arrived ten minutes later. It was excellent. The gratin was better. He ate slowly because the food deserved it and because every few minutes something would happen in the room — Lorri passing a table, Ginny laughing at something a customer said, Richard appearing at the kitchen door for two seconds to scan the room and then disappearing — and he wanted to watch.

The two women at the window had finished their meal and were now drinking coffee and talking in voices that kept dropping to murmurs and then rising into laughter. One of them had taken off her cardigan at some point and he couldn't have said when. The married couple was gone. A man his age had come in and taken the other end of the bar and Ginny was already talking to him like she'd known him for years, which maybe she had.

He looked at his notes. Address discrepancy. Unusual name. Limited menu. Pink lighting at noon. Co-owner chopping his own tarragon. Plant blocking a booth.

Nothing in his notes explained what he was feeling, which was that he'd walked into a restaurant and the restaurant had, very gently and without asking permission, walked into him.

"Dessert?" Ginny asked.

"What do you have?"

"Today? A chocolate pot de crème that Lorri made this morning, and my opinion on everything you've seen so far."

He closed his notebook. "I'll take both."

Ginny set the pot de crème in front of him. It was dark and simple and came in a white ramekin with a single mint leaf that was either garnish or commentary.

"So here's my opinion," Ginny said, leaning both hands on the bar. "You're going to go back to your desk and try to write a restaurant review. You're going to describe the menu and the lighting and the chicken, which was perfect, and you're going to mention the parking, which isn't. And none of it is going to explain this place."

"What would explain it?"

Ginny glanced toward the dining room, where Lorri was saying goodbye to the two women at the window. One of them touched Lorri's hand on the way out. It was a small thing. It was not a small thing.

"Come back for dinner," Ginny said. "Bring someone you like."

He looked at the booth behind the plant. The red leather caught the pink light and held it. He couldn't see if anyone was sitting in it.

He realized he wanted to know.

He also realized he'd stopped taking notes a while ago.

* * *

The Drive-In

Wayne called in April. He was planning to spend a weekend in the area, he said — actually he'd booked a room at Curtis House in Woodbury, a couple of nights — and thought we might find time to meet up.

"Are you bringing the Impala?" I asked.

"I was going to."

"There's a drive-in," I said. "Pleasant Valley. Twenty minutes from Middlebury through the Farmington River Valley. It's been there since 1955."

A pause. "You're suggesting we go to a drive-in."

"I'm observing that there's a drive-in and that you have a convertible and that the second weekend in May is usually warm enough."

"In the Impala."

"In the Impala," I confirmed.

Another pause — shorter this time. "What's playing?"

I'd already checked. "*Guardians of the Galaxy Vol. 3.*"

"That's a Marvel movie."

"It is."

"We're going to a Marvel movie at a drive-in in a 1960 Impala."

"Unless you have a better idea," I said.

He didn't have a better idea.

* * *

I should tell you about the skirt.

My daughter left clothes behind when she moved — the way daughters do, depositing layers of their former selves in closets that become a kind of archaeology project for the mothers who follow. Among the items, in a box on the top shelf: a cheerleader skirt and a halter top, vintage, from whatever era of her life those had belonged to.

I'd kept them because I keep things. Not hoarding — keeping. With the private intention that someday a thing might mean something different than it means today. I kept Colin's pension and turned it into a building. I kept thirty-three years of other people's kitchens and turned them into my own. I kept vinyl records from the DJ years and they're on the wall behind my bar. The skirt and the halter top had lived in their box for two years in my Ridgewood condo while I got on with other business.

And then one evening in May 2024, I was standing in front of my closet thinking about a drive-in date with a man who owned a 1960 Impala — the same car, the same man, a different drive-in — and I reached up and took the box down from the shelf.

The skirt fit. My daughter had hips. I have hips now. Different hips, same general circumference, forty years apart. It was light blue and white, pleated, the kind of skirt built for movement rather than modesty.

I held the halter top up to myself in the mirror. White, fitted, front-button. A sixty-year-old woman in her bedroom at Ridgewood, holding her daughter's clothes against herself, assessing the question. Not *can I* — that was answered. The question was: *will I.*

I thought about 1980. The Norwalk Drive-In, which no longer exists. Wayne at seventeen, nervous enough to be sweet about it. Whatever we'd done and hadn't done in the dark of that car, which I didn't remember precisely but remembered the feeling of — the feeling of being young and curious and at the beginning of something.

The Norwalk Drive-In was gone. But there was another drive-in. And there was the same man. And there was the same car, bought in 1980 and maintained with thirty-five years of upholsterer's hands.

I put on the halter top. I put on the skirt. I put on the custom bra from the shop on White Street in Danbury — the one built to specifications that most lingerie departments aren't equipped to discuss — because whatever else was happening tonight, I was going to be properly supported. White cotton panties, full-cut, newly purchased that week with the private awareness that this was a night that deserved new things. White crew socks. White tennis sneakers. The halter top buttoned over everything, concealing the rest.

Then I put on a wrap — light, covering — and looked at myself in the mirror.

Not seventeen. Not ridiculous. Not sad. A woman who had decided to have fun and raided the costume department to do it. My bare legs were visible below the wrap's hem. I left them that way.

I thought: *what if I showed up looking like the girl he would have taken to the drive-in in 1980.*

I thought: *he's going to lose his mind.*

I thought: *good.*

* * *

He picked me up at seven. The Impala sat in my driveway with the top up — sensible for an evening that might cool — the fire engine red of it vivid even in the early dusk, and I walked out to meet him with the wrap around my shoulders and my bare legs below and my secrets above.

Wayne was in clean dark jeans and a white dress shirt with the collar open. He looked at my legs.

"Nice evening for a drive," he said, with the expression of a man exercising deliberate restraint.

"Isn't it," I said, and got in.

* * *

The Pleasant Valley Drive-In has been on the same piece of ground since 1955, which in Connecticut terms means it has outlasted three generations of things that were supposed to outlast it. The screen is original. The speaker posts are still there, even though they also broadcast on FM now. The snack bar sells popcorn and Junior Mints and hot dogs and has not updated its menu or its aesthetic since approximately the Eisenhower administration, which is exactly right.

We paid at the gate and found a spot in the second row, center, and the radio was tuned to the broadcast frequency and the pre-show music came through the Impala's speakers and the sky went from blue to pink to dark while we talked about nothing in particular. Wayne's arm was along the back of the seat, not quite around my shoulders, in the manner of a man who has not yet established what his arm is permitted to do and is proceeding with appropriate caution.

Before the movie started he reached down and slid the bench seat back — a smooth rearward motion, unhurried.

"Sorry," he said. "When I redid the upholstery I modified the slide. More range than the original." He glanced at me. "Happy byproduct."

"Happy byproduct," I agreed.

And then I took off the wrap.

I'd timed it for the moment the lot was dark enough and the movie not yet started — the particular window of privacy that a drive-in affords between the last of the daylight and the first of the screen. I lifted the wrap from my shoulders and folded it onto the back seat and turned to face him.

Wayne looked at me.

The light blue and white pleated skirt. The white halter top and what the white halter top contained, which was visible in silhouette even before any buttons were opened. My bare legs. White socks, white sneakers. The whole ensemble assembled with full awareness of the effect and zero apology for it.

He looked at me the way the Impala looked at car shows — like something that had been worth keeping.

"Lorri," he said.

"I found it in a box," I said. "My daughter's. It fits."

"It fits," he confirmed, with feeling.

"I thought," I said, "that since we're doing the drive-in over, we might as well do it properly."

He looked at the skirt. At the halter top. At my legs. Then back at my face, with an expression that was equal parts delighted and overwhelmed and something quieter underneath that I recognized as the same feeling I'd had standing in front of my mirror an hour ago.

"You're something else," he said.

"So I've been told," I said. "Now put your arm around me. The movie's starting."

* * *

The movie was, as advertised, a Marvel movie — loud and colorful and operating at a frequency slightly above what the human nervous system strictly requires. Space raccoons. Elaborate action sequences. An emotional subplot about found family that I might have followed more closely under different circumstances. Wayne watched it with the comfortable attention of a man who can be entertained without being transported.

His arm was around my shoulders now. Properly. I was tucked against his side, his right arm warm across my back, and we watched the screen and the opening scenes did whatever opening scenes do when nobody is really watching them.

"Last time we did this," I said, "we were at Norwalk."

"'80. I was seventeen."

"Were you nervous?"

"Terrified," he said.

"You seemed very confident."

"I was performing confident," he said. "Completely different thing."

"And now?"

He considered this with appropriate seriousness. "Still terrified. Better at hiding it."

I laughed. On screen, something exploded. We ignored it.

His right hand, which had been resting on my shoulder, settled — a slow, unhurried arrival — against the top of the halter. Not grabbing, not pressing. Resting. The palm of a man who has decided this is where his hand belongs and is in no particular hurry to prove anything beyond that.

I didn't say anything. I watched the screen.

His hand stayed where it was.

The warmth of it traveled through the cotton. That was all, and it was sufficient — knowing what was underneath and what he knew was underneath and neither of us in any rush to renegotiate the terms of the evening. The raccoon on screen was having an emotional moment. Wayne's thumb moved, once, slightly. A small acknowledgment. Then still again.

"You're not watching," I said.

"I'm watching," he said.

"What just happened?"

A pause. "The raccoon said something."

"To whom?"

"To the... other one."

"There are several other ones."

"The blue one," he said, with some confidence.

I laughed and he laughed, and while we were laughing he turned toward me and kissed me.

Not a question. Not tentative. His mouth found mine with the intention of a man who has decided, and I kissed him back and felt the warmth of it travel from my mouth outward in every direction, the way warmth does when it's the right kind. His hand stayed on the halter throughout — warm, present, still — the kiss and the hand the same thing expressed in two places at once.

When we stopped, his forehead was against mine and we were both breathing slightly differently than before.

"Norwalk," I said. "Were you this good at Norwalk?"

"No," he said, without hesitation.

"What happened?"

"I was seventeen," he said. "I had no idea what I was doing."

"And now?"

"Still no idea," he said. "But I'm paying better attention."

He kissed me again — longer this time, with tongue, warm and unhurried, the kind of kiss that takes its time because it has decided it's going somewhere worth taking time over. His hand moved, very slightly, on the halter. Not rubbing. Just a small shift of weight, the palm learning the general geography of the territory without pressing for details. Enough to know. Enough to register the scale of things and go quietly still with that information.

We broke apart. On screen, something continued to happen to the raccoon.

"At Norwalk," I said, "did you have any idea?"

"Any idea of what?"

"This," I said, gesturing vaguely at the situation.

"No," he said. "I was seventeen. I thought you were pretty. I had no larger theory."

"And now you have a larger theory."

"Now I have," he said, his palm settling warm and deliberate against the front of the halter, "a working hypothesis."

I laughed. He kissed me again.

* * *

At some point — the movie was perhaps a third through — I shifted.

The pleated skirt is not engineered for sitting still. This is either a design flaw or a feature, depending on your circumstances, and my circumstances were a warm bench seat and a May evening and the specific awareness that I had chosen this skirt with full knowledge of what bench seats do to pleated hems. I moved, adjusting my weight, settling differently against the red leather.

The skirt moved with me. Considerably more than I had strictly intended, which was itself not entirely unintentional.

There was a pause.

"This," Wayne said, with great care, "never happened at Norwalk."

"We're not in Norwalk anymore," I said, and laughed — not the composed kind, the actual kind, the kind you can't schedule — and reached down and restored the skirt to a more defensible position, which took a moment because the pleats had opinions.

"You need help with that?" he said.

"You need to watch the movie," I said.

"The raccoon," he said, "will be fine."

I got the skirt sorted. Wayne's arm tightened slightly around my shoulders, warm and amused, and we sat in the particular companionable silence of two people who have just agreed on something without discussing it. His hand returned to the halter, resting there as before — warm, present, making no further case for itself. Both of us a little flushed. Both of us watching the screen with the diligent attention of people who are not watching the screen.

The raccoon was, in fact, fine.

* * *

We kissed through the second act and into the third. Not continuously — there was talking, and laughing, and at least one genuine exchange about whether space raccoons represented a metaphor for something, which we resolved inconclusively. But the kissing kept returning to itself, each time a little more certain than the last, his hand warm on the halter throughout, the cotton between his palm and everything beneath it a layer that neither of us moved to change. The evening had decided what it was. We had both agreed.

At some point the credits rolled. Neither of us had been tracking the ending.

The cars around us began their patient exit procession. We did not join it immediately. I found the wrap and settled it back around my shoulders, and Wayne watched me do this with the expression of a man cataloguing information he intends to keep.

"Better than Norwalk?" I said.

"There is no comparison," he said.

"We were seventeen."

"We were completely wasted on being seventeen," he said.

I looked at him. The smile lines. The steady warmth. The white dress shirt in the dark of the car, the dashboard light doing what dashboard light does to a face you're inclined to look at.

"Wayne," I said.

"Yes."

"You're still at the Curtis House tomorrow."

He looked at me. "I am."

"And I have a restaurant in Thornbury," I said, "with something I've been meaning to show you."

He waited.

"Come at seven-thirty," I said. "Leave the car at the Curtis House. It's a short walk."

He nodded. We joined the exit line and he drove me home through the Farmington River Valley with the May night moving past the windows. I had the window down because the window is always down. The spring air came through cold and clean and I thought about tomorrow with the particular quality of anticipation that belongs to a woman who has planned something and is looking forward to watching it land.

* * *

The Booth

He came to Amorous the next night.

I'd been dressed since six.

The gray hostess vest over the starched white blouse — cotton, tailored with darts that understood the assignment. The black bowtie at my collar. The garter belt and stockings and the custom bra from White Street in Danbury, doing what it always did. The four-inch heels. The things I was still learning to think of as a uniform, assembled with the intention of a woman who was beginning — slowly, without calling it that — to understand what she was building.

I sat in the office at six-fifteen and did paperwork I didn't need to do and listened to Martin finishing up in the kitchen and thought about the drive-in and thought about the booth and thought about the specific fact that I had never used this booth for this purpose — that tonight would be the first time — and felt, in my chest, the warm particular anticipation of someone standing at the beginning of something they can't quite name yet.

Ginny was behind the bar when I came out of the office. She looked at me — at the vest, at the bowtie, at the quality of attention I was giving the host stand — and set down her glass.

"Evening," she said.

"Evening."

She didn't say anything else. She didn't need to. Ginny had known about the kissing booths since before we opened — it had been part of the original conversation, the three of us around the office table with floor plans and wine, Richard asking practical questions and Ginny asking no questions at all, which meant she had already understood. The booths were built for this. Ginny had always known what they were for. She went back to her glass and I went back to the host stand and we both knew what we knew.

Wayne arrived at seven-thirty exactly.

He was in dark jeans and a white dress shirt again — the same combination as last night, or possibly a different version of it, the wardrobe of a man who has found something that works and applies it consistently. He looked at me from the host stand with the specific expression of a man who had spent the walk from the Curtis House to Main Street Thornbury thinking about last night and was now being confronted with a version of last night that had been upgraded.

The vest. The blouse. The bowtie.

"You look—" he started.

"Different," I said.

"I was going to say—"

"Come on," I said. "Ginny's got wine."

* * *

We sat at the bar and drank our wine and talked. About last night — obliquely, the way you discuss something that doesn't need direct discussion. About Curtis House, which he'd found comfortable. About the drive from Stamford that morning, the Farmington Valley in May, whether the Impala attracted attention on I-84 or whether people had stopped noticing remarkable things.

"They've stopped noticing," he said. "That's the problem with remarkable things. You have to be standing still for people to see them."

I looked at him over my wine glass.

"Speaking from experience?" I said.

"Speaking from thirty-five years of taking things to shows," he said, and smiled, and I thought: *he knows exactly what he just said.*

Ginny refilled our glasses without being asked. She was behind the bar and not looking at us, which is the position from which she sees everything.

After a while I said: "Let's sit somewhere comfortable." And I picked up both glasses and walked toward the corner.

He followed, and as he did he turned — a natural half-turn, unhurried — and took in the bar from across the room. The back-bar wall with its cubbies of vinyl, the bottles catching the amber light, the vintage amplifier glowing its quiet blue-green. The industrial pendants casting their focused pools on the dark wood below. Ginny in the half-shadow, polishing a glass, entirely unconcerned with being observed.

"You built that too," he said, still looking.

"Every inch," I said.

He turned back and followed me to the corner.

At the edge of the slatted screen I stopped and turned to him.

"Welcome," I said, "to my kissing booth. A restaurant named Amorous needed one — just because." I gestured toward the opposite corner. "I have two, actually. No waiting."

He looked at the booth — the red leather, the candle, the privacy of the screen and the plant and the drawn blinds — and then back at me, with the expression of a man who has just had a number of things confirmed simultaneously.

"Yours," he said.

"Mine," I said. "I built it that way on purpose. Now come in before the candle burns down."

* * *

I gestured for him to slide in first. He did. I settled to his left — close, the way you sit when close is the point — and his arm went around my shoulders and I let the warmth of it settle.

"You built all of this," he said.

"Thirty-three years of someone else's kitchens," I said. "Which turns out to be a very good foundation."

He nodded slowly, a man still assembling the picture. Then he turned to look at me. "You."

"Me," I said.

And then I said: "Let me get comfortable." And reached for the vest buttons.

Four of them. I took my time.

The vest opened and the sides fell away and the white blouse was there in the candlelight — the cotton, the darts, the structure visible now in a way the vest had not permitted. The top button still fastened. The bowtie at my collar. His eyes went to the blouse and I watched them go there and felt, in my chest, the particular satisfaction of a reveal landing the way it was meant to.

"The vest hid all of that," he said.

"That's what the vest is for," I said.

I reached up and untied the bowtie and set it on the table.

* * *

His arm was around my shoulders and the candlelight was doing its work and neither of us was looking at the room anymore. I turned toward him slightly and he understood the turn for what it was and kissed me — properly, without preamble, his mouth warm and certain. I kissed him back and felt the evening begin to find its shape.

We kissed for a while. The other tables in the restaurant were settling into their own evenings. Ginny was behind the bar being Ginny. The music played from the back-bar cubbies, something unhurried that she had selected with full intention and would describe, if asked, as having come up on shuffle.

His right hand moved from my shoulder — slowly, no drama — and settled against the front of the blouse. Flat. Warm. Present. His left arm stayed where it was, around my shoulders, drawing me in slightly as we kissed.

"The upholsterer," I said, "always needs to evaluate the fabric."

He went still for exactly one beat. "Oops," he said.

"Go ahead," I said. "I think I won't mind it at all."

He looked at me — the steady warmth of him, the smile lines deepening — and his right hand pressed gently against the blouse. The starched cotton gave slightly under the pressure, the cup beneath making itself known through the layer. He held that for a moment, simply registering, the way you register something you're glad to have confirmed.

"Different from last night," he said.

"Last night was a halter top at a drive-in," I said. "Tonight is a white blouse in a kissing booth. The upholsterer will note the distinction."

"The upholsterer notes the distinction," he confirmed, and kissed me again, his left arm pulling me gently closer while his right hand stayed warm and still against the blouse.

After a moment his right hand found a small ridge where the cotton had gathered slightly.

"There's a wrinkle," he said.

"I wonder how that happened," I said.

"I'll need to smooth it out."

"By all means," I said.

He smoothed it — carefully, with one hand, his left arm staying around my shoulders throughout. This took some time and produced another small wrinkle, which he also addressed with professional seriousness. I watched his face while he worked. The concentration of a craftsman engaged with materials he respects, and underneath it, barely contained, the expression of a man who finds the whole situation — the booth, the blouse, the woman in it — deeply and genuinely wonderful.

"More than our first date," he said.

"Much more," I said. "I figured you'd enjoy the difference."

He laughed — low and warm and entirely genuine — and kissed me with the specific delight of a man who has just discovered that the evening has even more to recommend it than he'd thought.

* * *

After a while his right hand left my blouse and found my knee.

I felt it there — warm through the skirt — and felt what was coming with the anticipatory awareness of a woman who had planned the leg sequence with the same care she'd planned the vest reveal. He pushed the skirt up slowly, the fabric sliding, and then his hand was on the stocking — the smooth nylon, the warmth of his palm through the weave.

He moved upward and found the stocking top.

He paused there. A real pause. Taking stock.

"I've been thinking about this," he said.

"I know," I said.

"Since last night."

"I know," I said again.

"You knew I'd been thinking about it."

"I dressed for it," I said.

His fingers traced the edge of the stocking top. Then found the garter strap — the small clip, the strap running upward — and followed it with one finger to where it met the belt, then back down, learning the route. His whole hand settled on my bare thigh above the stocking: skin on skin, warm and unhurried.

We kissed. His left arm drew me closer. His hand stayed on my thigh — present, warm, not moving toward anything further. Holding what it had found with the care of a man who understands that what he's been given is already more than enough.

He stayed there. Then, with the same unhurried quality that had governed the whole evening, his hand came back to my blouse.

We kissed between and during and throughout. His right hand warm through the cotton, his left arm steady around my shoulders. The specific conversation of his mouth and my chest — not a formula, a language. One that was, tonight, becoming fluent.

I filed this away. This was information. This was the beginning of something.

* * *

Time becomes irrelevant in the booth and then becomes relevant again all at once.

I became aware — gradually and then suddenly — that the restaurant had gone quiet. The other tables had cleared. Ginny was behind the bar in the amber light, doing the end-of-service things she does, the choreography of closing so practiced it requires no thought.

Wayne's hand was resting on my blouse, warm and still.

He looked at me. I looked at him. Neither of us said anything about what the evening had been, because it didn't need to be said.

"I should let you close up," he said.

"Probably," I said.

I buttoned the vest. Slowly. The vest covered the blouse. The bowtie stayed on the table.

He watched me button the vest the way he'd watched me open it — with the same expression, steadier now, the look of a man who has been given something to think about and is already thinking about it.

Ginny walked from the bar to the booth the way Ginny always walks — unhurried, watching. She arrived at the edge of the slatted screen and looked at the booth. One second. The open wine glasses. The bowtie on the table. Wayne's flushed face. My flushed face. The vest buttoned over the blouse.

The lipstick trace at the corner of Wayne's mouth. Small. She saw it.

She looked at me.

"Glasses," she said.

She cleared them. She went back to the bar.

* * *

Wayne left a few minutes later. We walked to the vestibule together and in the vestibule we kissed — one goodbye, and another, and a third that lasted long enough to make the first two seem like a preamble — and I stood in the doorway and watched him walk down Main Street toward the Curtis House in the May night, his hands in his pockets, unhurried.

I went back inside.

The restaurant was empty. Ginny was behind the bar, back to the room, finishing up. The record on the turntable turned slowly, finished, the arm returning to its rest. The back-bar sat in its amber shadow, the VU meters glowing their quiet blue-green.

I walked to the corner booth and sat down in it alone.

The candle was still lit — Ginny had left it. The seat was warm where Wayne had been. On the table, the slight ring-marks from the wine glasses, the bowtie I'd set down and not touched again. The slatted screen beside me, the plant in the corner, the blinds drawn against Main Street.

I sat in the booth I had built without knowing what I was building and looked at the room around it — the room I had assembled piece by piece from a thirty-year dream and a building I'd bought with a widow's resources and a clarity about what she wanted — and I thought about what had happened in this booth tonight.

Not the Electrician, last November. That night the booth was just the place we ended up. There had been no intention in it, no architecture — we'd moved to the booth because it was comfortable and private and the candle was lit, the way you sit somewhere because it's there and it's right, without understanding why it's right.

But tonight I had put Wayne in this booth on purpose. I had dimmed these lights on purpose. I had worn this vest and this blouse on purpose. I had seated myself to his left and let the evening proceed with the specific awareness — not quite a plan, not yet, but something directional — that this space was for this.

And it had worked. The booth had worked. The vest and the blouse and the plant and the screen and Ginny behind the bar with her clean sight line and her irreducible economy of response — all of it had worked the way things work when they've been built right, even if they were built for something else.

Glasses.

She had seen everything. She had said one word. She had cleared the glasses and gone back to the bar, and in doing so she had done exactly what this room required her to do, which was to see and know and keep and ask nothing in return.

I understood, sitting alone in the booth with the candle burning, that Ginny had just become something. Not tonight, exactly — she'd been becoming it since November, since the Electrician, since the night she'd turned off the bar lights and locked the front door and left the key on the bar without saying goodnight. But tonight something had been confirmed. She had walked to this booth and looked at it and said one word and gone back to her station, and in that sequence she had made herself the keeper of what happened here.

Not recruited. Not asked. She'd seen it, understood it, and chosen to do nothing with the knowledge except keep it. From tonight forward, Ginny knew what the booth was for.

I sat with this for a moment. The warmth of it. The specific comfort of having, without planning it, the right people in the right positions.

Wayne, who had walked from the Curtis House with his upholsterer's hands and his uncomplicated warmth, and who would come back. I knew this the way I knew the booth worked — not because anything had been promised, but because some things have a gravity.

The booth, which had been waiting, without knowing it was waiting, for exactly this.

Ginny, who would never say more than she'd said tonight, and didn't need to.

I blew out the candle. I put on my coat. I walked through the vestibule and out through the parking lot door and drove home to Ridgewood in the May night with the window down, because the window is always down, and the spring air came through and the road curved through the river valley and I thought about next time.

Not the specifics of it. Not the planning. Just the fact of it — that there would be a next time, and a time after that, and that each one would be built on the ones before it the way a good kitchen is built on thirty-three years of knowing what works and what doesn't.

I had a booth. I had a bartender who understood her role. I had a man who would come back from Stamford in a 1960 Impala because some things, once you've found them, you don't let go of.

I had more.

More had a room now.

That was enough.

That was everything.

* * *

The Drive Home

He sat in the car for a moment before turning the key.

Not thinking. Just sitting. The way you do when you've been somewhere and the somewhere is still on you and you're not ready to put the car in gear and make it the past tense.

Main Street was quiet. A few lights in the Curtis House behind him. The restaurant dark now, the parking lot empty. He could still feel the vestibule — the third goodbye, which had taken its time, which he had let take its time.

He turned the key. The engine came up, low and easy. He pulled out onto Main Street and headed south.

* * *

84 west to Danbury was highway, necessary, unremarkable. He gave it no thought. The Impala ran at sixty-five and Wayne drove with one hand on the wheel and let the road be what it was.

At Danbury he took the left onto Route 7.

The mall sat where the fairgrounds used to be. He didn't look at it directly — you never do, with those places. But he felt it as he passed, the way you feel ground that used to mean something. The Racearena had been there. Saturday nights, the Modified cars, the noise of it carrying across the whole valley. He'd been in those stands as a kid, shoulder to shoulder with every other teenager in Danbury who had nowhere better to be, which was nowhere better to be. The Fair in October. Paul Bunyan watching over all of it.

Gone now. Mall parking where the oval used to run.

He took the left and the mall fell away behind him and Route 7 became what it actually was — the road narrowing, the retail dropping off, the dark coming up on both sides. He'd driven this road his whole life. The bench seat held him the way it always had, the red leather broken in to the shape of a man who had been sitting in this seat since he was seventeen. He knew every sound the car made. Not by thinking. By years.

The road moved through Redding without announcing itself.

He knew whose town it was. He didn't dwell on it. He just drove through it the way you drive through a place that belongs to someone you're thinking about anyway.

Ridgefield came up — the main road, a restaurant on the corner he had no reason to notice. He bore right onto 35, then right onto 123, and the road changed immediately into something older. Stone walls. Horse farms set back in the dark. The kind of Connecticut that doesn't explain itself to anyone.

He drove it slowly. Nobody was waiting on him.

* * *

A working hypothesis, he'd told her at the drive-in. She'd laughed.

He hadn't been performing when he said it. He rarely performed. The line had arrived because it was true — because his hand had been on the halter and the halter had told him things about the evening's direction and a craftsman works from what the material tells him, not from what he'd planned to do before he touched it.

He thought about the booth.

The way she'd sat down and reached for the vest buttons without ceremony. Four buttons. Not rushing. The specific deliberateness of a woman who had thought about the order of things and was executing it at the pace she'd chosen. He'd watched her hands and understood, in the way he understood tension and seam and fit, that this was not improvisation. That she'd been here before, in her mind, well before he walked through the door.

He found this — he reached for the right word and located it — clarifying.

She'd built the whole thing. The restaurant, the booth, the lighting, the vest. The sequence. He'd walked from the Curtis House thinking he was coming for a drink and a conversation and discovered he'd been invited into something designed the way a good interior is designed — every element chosen, every proportion considered, nothing accidental.

He thought about the garter. The pause he'd taken when his hand found the stocking top. A real pause, because it deserved one.

I've been thinking about this.

I know.

She'd known. Of course she'd known. She'd dressed for it.

He thought: *she is something.*

He didn't elaborate. That was enough.

* * *

New Canaan came up on the hill — God's Acré, the white steeple catching whatever light the night offered, the green quiet below it. He'd passed this corner a hundred times. Tonight he noticed it.

Then down into Glenbrook. Her streets. He wasn't looking for anything. He just drove through them the way you drive through a place that belongs to someone, knowing it belongs to them, not stopping.

Stamford came up around the edges — the density of the exits, the particular light of a city that never entirely goes dark. He wound through streets he knew by feel, into the lot behind his building.

His parking spot. He pulled in and cut the engine.

The Impala went quiet. The tick of cooling metal. The lot empty at this hour, the building's windows mostly dark.

He sat for a moment. The same way he'd sat on Main Street in Thornbury before turning the key — bookending the drive. The car between then and now, holding both.

This car had been to the Norwalk Drive-In in 1980 with Lorri Ryan in the passenger seat. It had been to the Pleasant Valley Drive-In last night with the same woman in the same seat. He was fairly sure the car had an opinion about that. He was fairly sure it was the same opinion he had.

He got out. He locked it. He stood for a moment in the lot, looking at the car in the ambient light — the red of it dark and rich, the white top luminous.

Then he went inside.

He had things to think about. He was in no hurry.

* * *

Visit SomethingInTheWaterSeries.com

Learn more about Thornbury and what's coming next.

Scan to visit SomethingInTheWaterSeries.com

Also Available

Wayne — Book Three

Wayne comes back. He always comes back. But Lorri Oliver is sixty-one years old and Thornbury is changing and a man named Vincent Renzi just walked into Amorous on a Tuesday evening and sat down at the bar without asking for anyone.

About the Author

The Something In The Water series grew from a simple observation: that women of a certain age have stories that are funny and warm and occasionally breathtaking, and that nobody had been telling them quite right.

She lives in the Litchfield Hills of Connecticut.

Don't miss out!

Visit the website below and you can sign up to receive emails whenever Lorri Ryan Oliver publishes a new book. There's no charge and no obligation.

https://books2read.com/r/B-A-QKDNF-OCNHJ

BOOKS 2 READ

Connecting independent readers to independent writers.

Also by Lorri Ryan Oliver

Something In The Water
The Yearbook & The Impala
The Yearbook
The Impala
Wayne

Watch for more at https://somethinginthewaterseries.com/.

About the Author

Lorri Ryan Oliver has spent most of her adult life feeding people — first as a restaurant industry professional, and later as the owner of a small restaurant in a small Connecticut town that somehow became the center of a very large world.

She came to writing the way most people come to the things that matter — sideways, late, and wondering why it took so long.

The *Something In The Water* series grew from a simple observation: that women of a certain age have stories that are funny and warm and occasionally breathtaking, and that nobody had been telling them quite right.

She is doing her best to fix that.

Lorri lives in the Litchfield Hills area of Connecticut, where the autumn lasts exactly as long as it should and the coffee is always on and the stories never run out.

Read more at https://somethinginthewaterseries.com/.

www.ingramcontent.com/pod-product-compliance
Lightning Source LLC
LaVergne TN
LVHW090618110826
845146LV00001B/438

* 9 7 9 8 9 9 5 3 4 3 1 3 4 *